SIHA TOOSKIN KNOWS

The Offering of Tobacco

By Charlene Bearhead and Wilson Bearhead
Illustrated by Chloe Bluebird Mustooch

HIGHWATER PRESS

 Canada Council Conseil des arts
for the Arts du Canada

We acknowledge the support of the Canada Council for the Arts.
Nous remercions le Conseil des arts du Canada de son soutien.

HighWater Press gratefully acknowledges the financial support of the Province of Manitoba through the Department of Sport, Culture and Heritage and the Manitoba Book Publishing Tax Credit, and the Government of Canada through the Canada Book Fund (CBF), for our publishing activities.

HighWater Press is an imprint of Portage & Main Press.
Printed and bound in Canada by Friesens
Design by Relish New Brand Experience
Cover Art by Chloe Bluebird Mustooch

Library and Archives Canada Cataloguing in Publication

Title: Siha Tooskin knows the offering of tobacco / by Charlene Bearhead and Wilson Bearhead ; illustrated by Chloe Bluebird Mustooch.
Other titles: Offering of tobacco
Names: Bearhead, Charlene, 1963- author. | Bearhead, Wilson, 1958- author. | Mustooch, Chloe Bluebird, 1991- illustrator.
Identifiers: Canadiana (print) 20190058757 | Canadiana (ebook) 20190058781 | ISBN 9781553798460 (softcover) | ISBN 9781553798484 (PDF) | ISBN 9781553798477 (iPad fixed layout)
Classification: LCC PS8603.E245 S58 2020 | DDC jC813/.6—dc23

23 22 21 20   1 2 3 4 5

www.highwaterpress.com
Winnipeg, Manitoba
Treaty 1 Territory and homeland of the Métis Nation

I dedicate Siha Tooskin Knows the Offering of Tobacco *to my daughter Dakota. May you never stop giving and never stop receiving the gifts of knowledge. Embrace the gifts of life and live it to the fullest.*
—CHARLENE BEARHEAD

We dedicate the Siha Tooskin Knows series to the storytellers who taught us. To those who guided us and shared their knowledge so that we might pass along what we have learned from them to teach children. Their stories are a gentle way of guiding us all along the journey of life.

In that way we tell these stories for our children and grandchildren, and for all children. May they guide you in the way that we have been guided as these stories become part of your story.
—CHARLENE BEARHEAD AND WILSON BEARHEAD

Watch for this little plant!
It will grow as you read, and if you need a break,
it marks a good spot for a rest.

Paul Wahasaypa was a bit nervous as he walked towards Ms. Baxter's class at the end of the school day. He really liked his teacher and he couldn't imagine what she might want to see him about. She was very nice to him and was always interested in his ideas in class.

Paul was actually surprised by how much he liked his new school. He had been nervous about changing schools when his family moved here but it had turned out really well so far. The kids were very interested in learning about Paul and his people. He had thought maybe they would be unkind to him because there were not many Indigenous kids in this school, but so far so good. Today was unexpected though. This was the first time Paul had been asked to come back to Ms. Baxter's class after gym at the end of the day. He was racking his brain trying to think of what he might have done wrong. Well, he would soon find out as he had now arrived at the classroom door.

"Come in, Paul," Ms. Baxter called out when Paul stepped into the doorway. She motioned towards a chair at the table where she was sitting. A big stack of papers was clearly keeping her busy.

"Wow," thought Paul. "Maybe Ms. Baxter did something wrong. It sure looks like she is being punished. That's more homework than I've ever had." Ms. Baxter could almost read Paul's thoughts as she looked at his wide eyes staring at the big stack of papers waiting to be marked. "I know, right?" she laughed. "Good thing I like you guys so much or I'd really have to rethink this teaching thing. So much marking!"

The fact that Ms. Baxter was joking helped to ease Paul's mind a bit, but he still had to know what was going on. "Am I in trouble?" asked Paul as he walked towards the chair.

"Not at all," said his teacher with a reassuring smile. "I'm just hoping you can help me out a bit. I'm getting ready to teach the new science curriculum and I wanted to ask you about some things."

"Okay," Paul answered, a little confused. He was pretty good at science but he had never been asked to help with the curriculum before.

"Many times when we are learning things in class you have such interesting information to share. I often hear you talk about how you've learned these things from people in your family. I was thinking it would be awesome to have all of our students learn from some of your teachers, but I wanted to ask you first." Paul listened with interest. He still wasn't sure what Ms. Baxter wanted his help with, but it sounded intriguing. "Do you think it would be okay to ask your grandparents to come in to teach us some things that we should all know?"

Paul was surprised but really excited. He was very aware that Mitoshin and Mugoshin knew many

things, but he was surprised that his teacher had figured that out.

Paul's grandparents had taught him so many things, but he had never really thought of them as teachers. He just knew that they were amazing.

"That would be great," Paul replied. "I think it would be so cool to have Mitoshin and Mugoshin come in to teach our class. Uhm…but you'd have to ask *them*."

"That's why I need your help, Paul," Ms. Baxter continued. "I don't know much about Nakota protocols but I know that I want to learn. I know that there are certain ways to approach an Elder. I was told that I should offer tobacco. Is that the right way to do things with your grandparents?"

"Well," Paul began, "That is what we do in my family when we want to ask someone for help. You are asking Mitoshin and Mugoshin if you can talk to them about sharing what they know so offering tobacco is a good start."

"Actually," Paul added with a nod of approval, "I'm really impressed that you understand that offering tobacco doesn't mean you are promoting smoking. Many non-Indigenous people get all freaked out when they hear 'offering tobacco' because they start to lecture us about the health hazards of smoking. Mugoshin says we need to tell them about the sacred use of tobacco. It's the plants that we are offering for use in ceremony and not cigarettes. You are already ahead of the game because you know what it really means." Ms. Baxter beamed a little as Paul praised her.

"When my mom and Mugoshin take me out to pick berries in the summer we always put down tobacco and thank Ena Makoochay and the berries for giving us food to keep us healthy," Paul continued. "Ena says that we never take anything from Ena Makoochay without giving something back, so we offer tobacco."

Paul noticed that his teacher looked a little bit confused and he realized that she didn't understand Nakota. "Oh yeah," he said with a little grin, "'Ena Makoochay' means 'mother earth' in our language. 'Ena' is 'mother' or 'mom.' 'Mitoshin' is 'my grandpa,' and 'Mugoshin' is 'my grandma.'"

"Thanks," smiled Ms. Baxter. "You almost lost me there for a minute."

"No problem," replied Paul with an understanding nod. "There are lots of things we can teach each other. That's what Mugoshin always says. She teaches me lots of things. When we go

to pick sweetgrass Mugoshin reminds me that we should never pull plants out by the roots because that will kill them. She tells me that plants have families too and if we pull them out of the ground that will be the end of their family. Mugoshin lets me put down some tobacco too so we can both thank Ena Makoochay for the gifts she gives to us. The tobacco is also a gift that we give to the sweetgrass family in return for their gift to us. Mugoshin says that I teach her patience when we are braiding the sweetgrass."

Paul laughed. "I think that is a nice way of saying I'm slow and my sweetgrass braids aren't the most even and beautiful ones in the bunch. I keep trying though. Mugoshin says that's how we learn."

"That is such a beautiful and important teaching, Paul," Ms. Baxter said with an appreciative nod. "You actually just taught me something important that I will need to include in our science lessons about plants. Maybe you should be teaching that part. You really have a lot of knowledge for an 11-year-old."

"Thanks Ms. Baxter," Paul replied. He was happy that he could help. "Ena says that we are all students and we are all teachers. We need to listen and watch to learn from the people who take time to teach us and we need to share what we learn with others so that we can all live together in a good way, because everything has a life and a spirit. My parents and grandparents always remind me that we never ask for something without giving back. They say that's the way of our people, and offering tobacco was one of the ways that was given to us to do that."

"The other thing you need to think about is what you are actually asking for," Paul explained further. "I know you want Mugoshin and Mitoshin to teach about science, but that would take them all day, every day, for the whole year and we still wouldn't be finished. When you offer someone tobacco you have to say what you are asking for so they can decide if they will accept the tobacco or not. Different people have different knowledge. An Elder won't accept the tobacco if they don't have the knowledge that you are asking for. They will guide you to the person you need to ask."

"That's really good to know, Paul. There is so much to learn, but I'll start with the units that make the most sense to ask your grandparents about. Do you have any suggestions?" Ms. Baxter was eager to hear more.

"Well, I know that Mitoshin knows a lot about the stars. You could ask him to teach us about that. Things like the star formations and where they are in the sky at different times of the year. I am only starting to learn so I'm not much help there. I need to learn more about that myself," Paul admitted. "At this point I can only tell you that if you can't see the stars at night then it's cloudy." They both chuckled.

"But seriously," Paul added, "Mitoshin has told me stories about how our people used the stars to guide them when they were moving their villages at different times of the year."

"Mugoshin could teach us about plants and the water. I know we are supposed to learn about wetlands this year in science," Paul continued. "I don't know a lot about that yet either but Mugoshin tells me that the wetlands are like Ena Makoochay's kidney. I don't know everything about the human kidney or the wetlands, but I know it has something to do with the plants in

the wetlands cleaning the water the same way the human kidney cleans our blood."

"I'm impressed, Paul," Ms. Baxter proclaimed. "That's two of our science units already. This is so exciting. I will be learning as much as all of my students if we can get your grandparents to come in and teach us."

"One of the things that I am learning about from Mitoshin is forest farming." Paul beamed with pride.

"What is forest farming?" Ms. Baxter asked, showing genuine interest. "Is that like tree farming where farmers plant trees in rows and grow them to sell?"

"Not exactly," Paul explained. "Mitoshin says that he hears non-First Nations people call it 'forest management,' but he says we can't really manage something that is more powerful than us. Mitoshin is teaching me about how our people used to select a place in the forest where the right type of trees are growing for a particular purpose. There is much to learn about how to clean out unwanted plants from the area, remove unwanted branches, and lots of other steps to give the trees the environment that they need to grow to a certain size and a certain shape."

"That's amazing!!!" Ms. Baxter exclaimed. She looked even more impressed.

"I know," agreed Paul. "Mitoshin reminds me to think about these things logically. He asks me questions like, 'Do you actually think that our ancestors would wander around for weeks and months in hopes of finding just the right tree for a canoe or a bow?'"

Ms. Baxter and Paul looked at one another for a moment then both shrugged their shoulders. "Good point," noted Ms. Baxter. "There's so much for me to learn that I don't know where to start."

"Just think about what you want to ask. My grandparents can guide you from there if they have time and agree to visit our school to share their teachings." Paul was full of suggestions.

"Wow," said Ms. Baxter with a sigh of relief. "I sure came to the right person for advice. I have already talked to the principal about the budget. It's important that we pay people for their time when they come to teach at a school. I can handle the part about how we pay people to teach us things, but you know what I need to do when I go out to ask Elders, Knowledge Keepers, or other community members for help. We make a good team, Paul.

Now I'd better call your mom to see if she can help me set up a time to meet Mitoshin and Mugoshin."

"That sounds good," Paul replied. "Also, I'll teach you a little more Nakota before you call because you just called them your grandpa and grandma. You should say 'Nitoshin' and 'Nigoshin' because that means 'your grandpa' and 'your grandma.'" Paul laughed as Ms. Baxter shook her head and covered her mouth with one hand.

"That is possible, though," Paul said with a smile. "Adoption is a practice for our people as well, but I'll tell you more about that on another day."

"That sounds like a good deal, Paul," Ms. Baxter replied as she smiled and held out her hand to shake Paul's hand in agreement. "In the meantime I'll practice the Nakota words that you taught me today and get my tobacco ready to offer Nitoshin and Nigoshin. I'd better let you get going or your mom will be calling me to see what is taking you so long."

"And I'd better let you get back to your marking, Ms. Baxter," Paul agreed. "By the way, you might want to talk to Mitoshin and Mugoshin about oral tradition as well. If you started teaching the way our people always did, the students would all have to work harder to remember what we learned. On the plus side, you would have a lot less marking to do."

Glossary

Ade	Dad or father
Ena	Mom or mother
Ena Makoochay	Mother earth
Mitoshin	My grandfather
Mugoshin	My grandmother
Nigoshin	Your grandmother
Nitoshin	Your grandfather
Siha Tooskin	Little Foot (siha is foot; tooskin is little)
Wahasaypa	Bear head

A note on use of the Nakota language in this book series from Wilson Bearhead:

The Nakota dialect used in this series is the Nakota language as taught to Wilson by his grandmother, Annie Bearhead, and used in Wabamun Lake First Nation. Wilson and Charlene have chosen to spell the Nakota words in this series phonetically as Nakota was never a written language. Any form of written Nakota language that currently exists has been developed in conjunction with linguists who use a Eurocentric construct.

ABOUT THE AUTHORS

Charlene Bearhead is an educator and Indigenous education advocate. She was the first Education Lead for the National Centre for Truth and Reconciliation and the Education Coordinator for the National Inquiry into Missing and Murdered Indigenous Women and Girls. Charlene was recently honoured with the Alumni Award from the University of Alberta and currently serves as the Director of Reconciliation for *Canadian Geographic*. She is a mother and a grandmother who began writing stories to teach her own children as she raised them. Charlene lives near Edmonton, Alberta with her husband Wilson.

Wilson Bearhead, a Nakota Elder and Wabamun Lake First Nation community member in central Alberta (Treaty 6 territory), is the recent recipient of the Canadian Teachers' Federation Indigenous Elder Award. Currently, he is the Elder for Elk Island Public Schools. Wilson's grandmother Annie was a powerful, positive influence in his young life, teaching him all of the lessons that gave him the strength, knowledge, and skills to overcome difficult times and embrace the gifts of life.

ABOUT THE ILLUSTRATOR

Chloe Bluebird Mustooch is from the Alexis Nakoda Sioux Nation of central Alberta, and is a recent graduate of the Emily Carr University of Art + Design. She is a seamstress, beadworker, illustrator, painter, and sculptor. She was raised on the reservation, and was immersed in hunting, gathering, and traditional rituals, and she has also lived in Santa Fe, New Mexico, an area rich in art and urbanity.